James Leach

I Love Wheels

FOLLETT DOUBLE SCOOP BOOKS

The Troll Family Stories
  Hi, Dog!
  A Dog Is Not a Troll
  Go, Wendall, Go!
  I Love Wheels
  Etta Can Get It!
  A Troll, a Truck, and a Cookie

Other series of Follett Double Scoop Books:
The Cora Cow Tales
The Adventures of Pippin

I Love Wheels

Phylliss Adams
Eleanore Hartson
Mark Taylor

Illustrated by Dennis Hockerman

Follett Publishing Company
Chicago, Illinois

Atlanta, Georgia • Dallas, Texas
Sacramento, California • Warrensburg, Missouri

LC 81–17413
ISBN 0–695–41615–4
ISBN 0–695–31615–X (pbk.)

"Look, Blossom," said Buddy.
"See the wheels."

"I love wheels!" said Blossom.

5

"We love wheels," said Blossom. "And we want to ride."

"Can we ride this?" said Buddy.

"Jump up, Buddy," said Blossom.
"Jump up and ride."

"Here I come," said Buddy.

"I love wheels!" said Blossom.

7

"Here we come," said Buddy.

"Go, go, go," said Blossom.
"I love wheels."

"Look, Blossom," said Buddy.
"I see wheels!"

"I want to ride," said Blossom.
"I <u>have</u> to ride.
I love wheels!"

"Can we ride it?" said Buddy.

"Buddy and I love wheels,"
said Blossom.

10

11

12

"I can not ride this," said Blossom.
"And I love to ride.
I love wheels!"

13

"Jump in, Blossom," said Buddy.
"We can ride in this."

"I love it," said Blossom.
"I love it!"

Up!

Up!

Up!

Down!

Down!

Down!

17

"I <u>have</u> to ride this,"
said Blossom.

"This is not the ride I want,"
Blossom said.

18

"Look, Buddy," said Blossom.

"See the wheels."

"Here we come," said Buddy.

"And we have wheels,"
said Blossom.
"Wheels, wheels, wheels!"

FIRE
STATION

21

"Hi," said Buddy.

"We have wheels," said Blossom.

"We see," said Leona and Wendall.

"Wheels," said Buddy.
"Wheels, wheels, wheels."

"I love wheels," said Blossom.

"Wheels!" said Etta.

The Troll Word Book

have I <u>have</u> wheels.

here <u>Here</u> I come.

in Dandy Dog can not get <u>in</u> this.

jump　　See Blossom <u>jump</u>.

ride　　Buddy and Blossom love to <u>ride</u>.

we　　<u>We</u> can play.

Wheels! Wheels! Wheels!

Point to each toy and name it.
Then find the missing wheel for the toy.

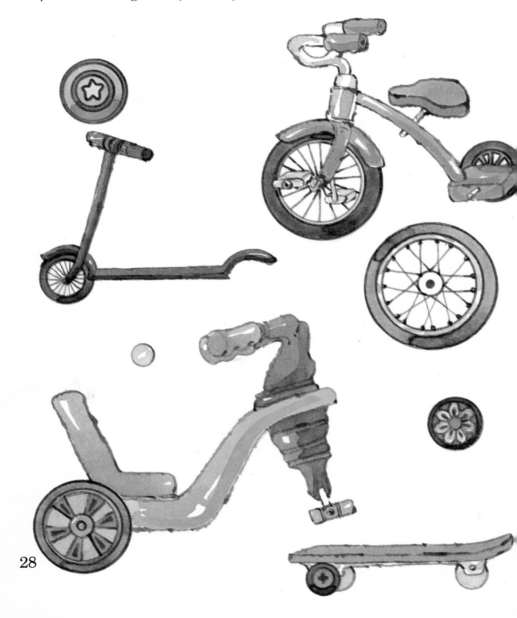

28

We Have It Here!

Look at the green stand.
Point to and name the things you can play with.
Look at the red stand.
Point to and name the things you can eat.

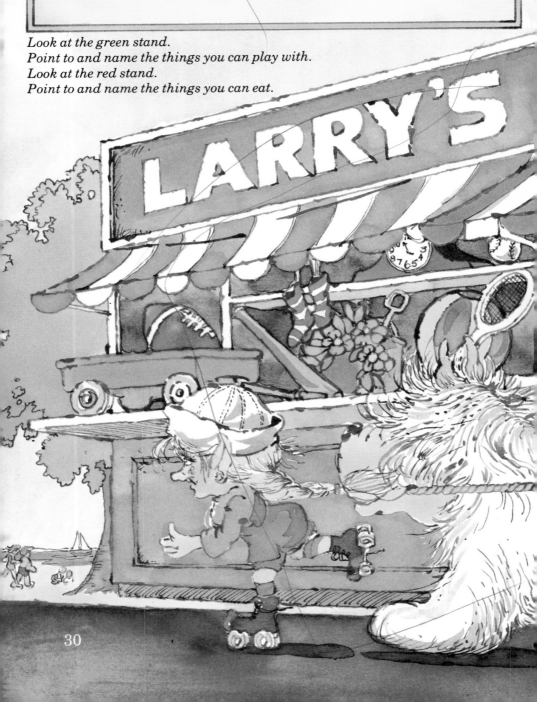

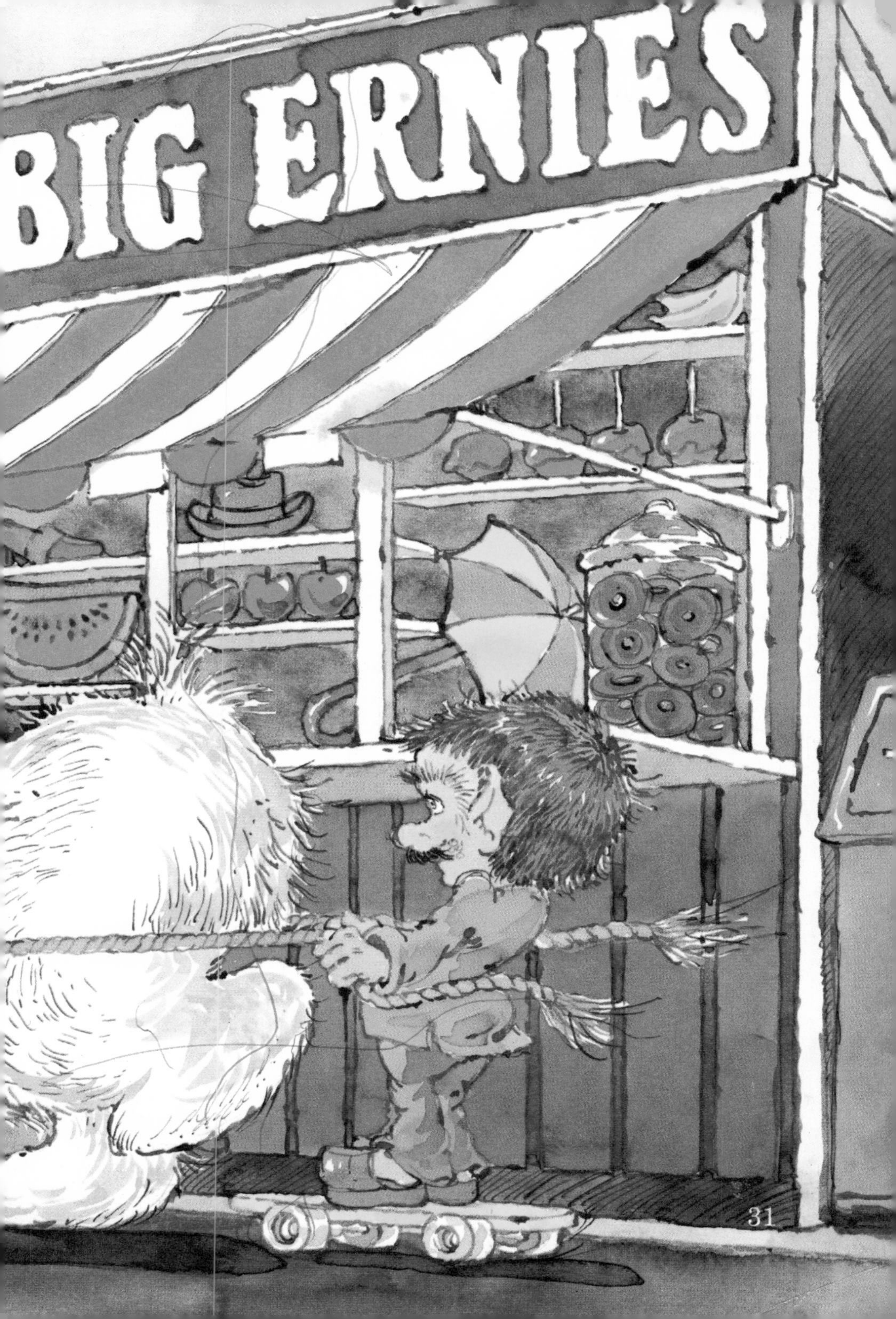
BIG ERNIE'S

I Love Wheels is the fourth book of the Troll Family Stories for beginning readers. All words used in the story are listed here. (The words in darker print were introduced in this book. The other words were introduced in earlier books.)

and	go	**jump**	the
Blossom	**have**	Leona	this
Buddy	**here**	look	to
can	hi	**love**	up
come	I	not	want
down	**in**	**ride**	**we**
Etta	is	said	Wendall
	it	see	**wheels**

About the Authors

Phylliss Adams, Eleanore Hartson, and Mark Taylor have a combined background that includes writing books for children and teachers, teaching at the elementary and university levels, and working in the areas of curriculum development, reading instruction and research, teacher training, parent education, and library and media services.

About the Illustrator

Since his graduation from Layton School of Art in Milwaukee, Wisconsin, Dennis Hockerman has concentrated primarily on art for children's books, magazines, greeting cards, and games.

The artist lives and works in his home in Mequon, Wisconsin, with his wife and two children. The children enjoyed many hours in their dad's studio watching as the Troll Family characters came to life.

123456789/8685848382